PRESERVING
MY PRETTY

Fighting for Life, Love and Legacy

Angela Denise Daniels-Gray, MSW

TABLE OF CONTENTS

AUTHOR'S NOTE

There are some stories we carry quietly, not because they lack importance, but because the weight of speaking about them out loud feels too heavy to hold. For years, mine lived tucked inside my heart, whispered in pieces, shared only with the few people who had earned that level of trust.

But healing has a strange way of showing up with a mirror and a calling. It reminds you that your story isn't just about you. It's about the women who will see themselves in your survival. It's about the mothers, daughters, sisters, caretakers, survivors, and thrivers who are still trying to make sense of their own reflections. It's about every person searching for beauty beneath their wounds, strength beneath their scars, and hope in the middle of their hardest seasons.

I did not write this book because my journey has been perfect. I wrote it because it's honest.

Painful.

Beautiful.

Transformative.

Human.

This book is my offering, a place where I lay down the pieces of my story so you can pick up the pieces of your own. A space where truth is not something to fear but something to honor. A reminder that "pretty" is not lost in the battles we fight, it simply shifts, deepens, and reveals itself in new ways.

As you read, I ask one thing of you:

Be gentle with yourself.

Turn these pages slowly.

Let each chapter meet you where you are.

Write what needs to be written.

Release what needs to be released.

And allow yourself the grace to heal in your own time, in your own way.

Thank you for holding my story with care.

Thank you for allowing this book to speak to your heart. And thank you, truly, for being here.

With all my love,

Angela

INTRODUCTION

Preserving My Pretty: Fighting for Life, Love, and Legacy

There comes a moment in every woman's life when she realizes she is no longer fighting the world; she's fighting for herself. For her peace. For her joy. For her voice. For the parts of herself she once dimmed or dismissed just to survive.

This book was born in one of those moments for me.

When I heard the words "You have breast cancer," time itself shifted. Suddenly, life felt sharp, fragile, and unbearably honest. I wasn't just battling a diagnosis; I was facing every layer of myself. The parts of me I had neglected. The pain I had tucked away. The lessons I inherited. The love I had given. The love I withheld, even from myself.

This memoir is my story, raw, imperfect, beautiful, and real. But it isn't *only* a story. It's a companion. A safe place. A guided journal meant to walk with you through your own moments of healing, awakening, and becoming.

At the end of each chapter, you'll find:

- Reflection prompts to help you explore your experiences with honesty and compassion

- Affirmations to remind you of your strength, worth, and resilience

- Space to write, breathe, release, and reconnect with yourself

Because healing isn't just about what happened to us, it's about who we become after.

You don't have to be a survivor to feel this book. You don't have to have battled breast cancer, grief, or heartbreak. You only need to be a woman who wants to grow, who wants to understand herself on a deeper level, or who wants to "preserve her pretty" in a world that tries to take it from her.

My hope is that these pages make you feel seen, held, and empowered. That you discover parts of your story you didn't know were waiting to be acknowledged. That, as you read my journey, you feel safe enough to face yours.

Thank you for letting me share my heart. Now I invite you to share yours.

Let's heal.

Let's grow.

Let's preserve our pretty, TOGETHER!

DEDICATION

This book is dedicated to my son, David. My heartbeat, my answered prayer, and my greatest reason to fight. You are the light that guided me through every dark season, the joy that reminded me I had something worth living for, and the proof that hope truly is hereditary. Thank you for loving me through every version of myself, for forgiving the moments when I was breaking, and for growing with me as I learned how to rebuild. You are my legacy, my purpose, and my forever miracle.

To my mother and father, thank you for giving me life, and for the lessons your love and loss left behind. Your stories are woven into every page.

To my Aunt Essie, my first protector, and to my Grandpa, whose wisdom still walks with me. Thank you for teaching me strength long before I knew I would need it.

And to every little girl born in a storm who had to fight her way into the light, this book is for you. For the ones who learned to love themselves in pieces, who survived what could have broken them, and who are still becoming despite everything. May you always remember that your beginnings do not define you. Your becoming does!

ACKNOWLEDGMENTS

To my family and friends, thank you for being my village when I needed one most.

To my sisters, cousins, and girlfriends who researched treatments, delivered meals, bought comfort gifts, and made me laugh through the hardest days. You carried me through healing in ways I can never repay.

To my son's father and his family, thank you for stepping in with love, care, and consistency. You helped me hold life together when it was trying to fall apart.

To Mrs. Kennedy ("Sista") and her husband, thank you for believing in a young girl from Jersey City who just wanted to run. Your guidance and encouragement changed the trajectory of my life.

To Ms. Victoria, thank you for your light, your courage, and the inspiration you poured into my heart. You remain part of the foundation of Pink Hope.

To Cousin (Marjorie), thank you for loving me, laughing with me, and growing with me. Your memory strengthens me every day.

To Uncle Chuck, thank you for your wisdom, your warmth, and your unwavering belief in me. Your questions, your pride, and your presence are still with me.

To Fajr, the brave little warrior whose joy outshined her pain, thank you for teaching the world that strength can come in the smallest, brightest packages. Your light continues to guide more than you could ever know.

To my colleagues in crisis response, thank you for reminding me daily that empathy is power, and that helping others heal is one of the most sacred honors of all.

To my therapist, thank you for offering me a safe space to unravel, rebuild, and learn to breathe again. Your wisdom, thoughtful assignments, and gentle honesty helped me confront the pain I had avoided for years. Thank you for reminding me that I deserve grace, rest, and compassion, not just from others, but from myself.

To every survivor, thriver, caretaker, and believer who has crossed my path, thank you. Your stories remind me that beauty, strength, and hope are still alive in this world.

And to God. Thank you for walking with me through every shadowed valley and carrying me through seasons I didn't think I'd survive. Thank You for loving me back to myself, for restoring my faith, and for never letting go of me, even when I let go of You. Every victory in this book is a reflection of Your grace.

ABOUT THE AUTHOR

Angela Denise Daniels-Gray is a mother, survivor, advocate, and the heart behind *Pink Hope*, a movement devoted to reminding women that beauty, strength, and identity are never lost, even in life's hardest seasons.

Born and raised in Jersey City, NJ, resilience has shaped Angela's journey from the beginning. She has lived through childhood trauma, family loss, single motherhood, divorce, and a battle with stage 3, triple-positive breast cancer. Experiences that not only tested her but transformed her. Through every valley, she discovered a deeper purpose, unshakable faith, and the power of healing from the inside out.

For more than two decades, Angela has worked in the helping profession and has spent nearly a decade serving as a crisis responder, supporting individuals during their most vulnerable moments. Her lived experience, grounding presence, and extraordinary capacity for empathy allow her to hold space for others with compassion and strength.

Her breast cancer journey inspired the creation of Pink Hope Boutique, a brand dedicated to helping women reclaim their confidence, style, and sense of self during and after treatment. This blossomed into the Pink Hope Foundation, a community-centered initiative offering emotional, mental, and spiritual support to survivors, thrivers, and caretakers. Through these efforts, Angela honors the legacy of Victoria, a beloved mentor and friend, as well as the women who cared for her along the way.

Today, Angela uses her voice to uplift others through storytelling, advocacy, and community work. Her mission is simple yet powerful: to remind every woman that she is still beautiful, still worthy, and still becoming. No matter what life has taken her through.

When she's not writing or advocating, Angela finds joy in motherhood, self-care, and creating spaces where healing, hope, and sisterhood thrive.

She believes deeply that: Even after the deepest heartbreaks, hope always finds a way, especially Pink Hope.

PROLOGUE
THE DAY I CHOSE TO LIVE

I remember the way my thoughts went silent. The lab tech was talking on the other end of the phone, but all I could hear was the echo of my heartbeat. The air felt thick, heavy, almost unbreathable.

"Angela… your labs were positive for breast cancer. Your doctor will call you." *Click.*

I didn't cry. I didn't scream. I just stared at the road and drove to a nearby park.

My first thought wasn't dying; it was my son. His face, his smile, his future. How would I tell him? How would I protect him from the fear already wrapping itself around my chest?

In that moment, my life split into "before" and "after."

The "before" held a lifetime of battles I had already survived. The "after" was demanding a different kind of strength.

The first person I called was my son's father. I couldn't form the words without breaking, but he steadied me, reminding me that our son needed me and so did he. My next call was my cousin, who cried with me and spoke hope into the cracks forming in my spirit.

Then my phone rang. It was Ms. V. She had become more than a nail tech; she was a sister, a voice of wisdom, a woman who had faced cancer twice and still radiated grace. After I told her the news, she went quiet, then said, "Start fighting now, Angela. Don't wait until the treatments. Don't wait until you're scared. Start fighting before it starts."

And something shifted.

I realized survival was more than medicine, more than statistics. It was a mindset. Faith. Willpower. It was choosing life even when everything felt uncertain.

That day, I decided this would not be the end of my story.

I was going to fight, not just to live, but to *live beautifully*.

To protect the parts of me that trauma tried to steal.

To preserve my peace, my purpose, and my pretty.

Life taught me something breast cancer could never erase:

I come from struggle, but I'm not defined by it.

I come from loss, but I carry love.

And even when everything falls apart, I still have hope. Pink Hope.

That was the day I chose to live.

Not to exist.

Not to endure.

But to reclaim the woman I was always meant to become.

For Your Reflection

1. Can you remember a moment when your life split into a "before" and "after"?

_____

_____

_____

2. When you receive hard news, who is the first person you want to call, and why are they safe?

_____

_____

_____

3. What does "choosing to live" look like for you today, emotionally, spiritually, or physically?

_____

_____

_____

Affirmations to Hold Onto

- I honor the moments that could have broken me and celebrate that I am still here.

- Even in fear, I am allowed to choose life, hope, and healing.

PART I

INTRODUCTION: ROOTS

Before we can talk about healing, we must speak of where the hurt began. Part I is the story of my beginnings, the people who shaped me, the homes that held me, and the wounds that were planted before I ever understood their weight. In these chapters, I return to the places where love and loss lived side by side, where chaos and comfort intertwined, and where I first learned what it meant to survive. These roots, both tender and tangled, formed the foundation of everything I would one day become.

Some Beginnings Feel Like Storms, But Storms Teach You How To Stand.

Chapter 1
BORN INTO THE STORM

Before I knew what pain or struggle was, I knew Aunt Essie.

She was the first person who made me feel safe. My first protector. My first definition of beauty. I can still see her now, tall, elegant, dressed in fabulousness even on an ordinary Tuesday. Her perfume always entered the room before she did, soft and floral, unforgettable. To me, she was everything a mother was supposed to be.

Before I went to live with my grandfather, I lived with her. I must've been three or four, too young to understand the complicated reasons adults make the choices they make, but old enough to know that Aunt Essie loved me. She brushed my hair every morning, called me her beautiful ladybug, as if it were my given name, and told me stories about women who survived things meant to break them. In my little world, she was magic, and I was her girl.

When we moved in with Grandpa, everything felt different. His world was different; he was legally deaf and blind, yet he had been approved to care for three girls. My oldest sister went to live with her father, a man I would later learn was also mine. I stayed with Grandpa, his "Babygirl," as he called me, and he loved me in his own gentle, steady way. But even with that, I missed Aunt Essie every single day. I remember asking when she would visit and receiving only silence, the kind that makes a child feel something is wrong even without words.

Not long after, she died. Sclerosis of the liver, they said, words I didn't understand, but I understood heartbreak. I cried when they told me I couldn't attend her funeral. I didn't understand why. I just knew someone who made me feel loved was gone, and I had no way to say goodbye.

Later, I overheard the adults whispering that she had left everything to me. To a child, that meant she must have loved me deeply. But whatever "everything" was, I never saw it. What I did hold onto was her voice, her laugh, and the way she made me feel. Maybe that was worth more than anything she could've left behind.

Years later, I told my mother that for a long time, I believed Aunt Essie was my real mom. I still remember the way her face changed to anger, maybe pain, maybe guilt. I hadn't meant to hurt her. I was simply telling my truth. But the truth has a way of reopening wounds people never tended to in the first place.

Even now, when I think about love, I think about Aunt Essie. She was the first person who saw me before I even knew who I was. She taught me that "pretty" wasn't about clothes or hair or appearance, it was about how you were loved and protected. And when she left, I learned my first lesson about loss.

Sometimes love teaches you how to be strong by leaving you too soon.

For Your Reflection

1. Who was the first person in your life who made you feel truly safe or seen? What did they do that made you feel that way?

_____

_____

_____

2. What early losses or changes shaped how you understand love today?

_____

_____

_____

3. Are there things you were "too young to understand" that you now see more clearly as an adult? How have they affected you?

_____

_____

_____

Affirmations to Hold Onto

- I am worthy of the kind of love that protects, nurtures, and sees me.

- My beginnings may have been chaotic, but they do not define my worth.

Love Doesn't Need Perfect Words; Sometimes It Speaks Through Presence Alone.

Chapter 2
THE HOUSE WHERE I LEARNED TO LISTEN

After Aunt Essie was gone, the world slowed down. The shuffle of my grandfather's slippers replaced the laughter and perfume that used to fill the air moving through the house. He was blind, but somehow, he always knew exactly where I was.

"Morning, baby," he'd say, turning his head toward the sound of my footsteps. His voice carried both gravel and grace, the kind of voice that made you feel like everything was going to be okay, even when it wasn't.

Grandpa was born in 1918, the grandson of a slave. He had very little education, couldn't read or write, yet he understood life in a way that felt bigger than books. He grew up in Georgia, where his mother worked as a sharecropper, and he'd tell me stories about fields that stretched as far as he could feel. When his sister married an older man, a decision that kept their family together, they eventually relocated to Jersey City, NJ. Those stories didn't come from textbooks; they lived in the cadence of his voice, the pauses between memories, the history woven into the things he chose to share.

He couldn't read to me, but he taught me. He taught me my numbers, how to count change, and how to tell one coin from another by touch alone.

"Feel it, baby," he'd say, rolling a nickel or penny between my fingers. "Each one has its own sound. You just got to listen." He'd drop them on the table one by one so I could hear the difference: the soft ring of a dime, the solid thud of a quarter. That's how I learned, by sound, by touch, by trust.

He wore a hearing aid that whistled whenever he bent over his coffee. I used to giggle at that sound, and he'd smile and say, "That's just the world trying to talk to me." Even after everything life had taken from him, his sight, his hearing, the certainty of an easy life, his humor never dimmed.

We didn't have much, but I never felt poor in Grandpa's house. The radio was our window to the world, with gospel music and Sunday sermons humming softly in the background. He couldn't see the sunlight pouring through the curtains, but he'd hum like he could feel it on his skin. In that small home, I learned patience. I learned rhythm. I learned that love didn't always sound like "I love you." Sometimes it sounded like, "Come here, let me show you again."

Looking back, Grandpa gave me a kind of armor I didn't yet know I'd need. Aunt Essie taught me that I was beautiful. Grandpa taught me that I was capable.

Between the two of them, I was quietly prepared for a world that would test every lesson they gave me. A world that would demand strength, grace, and a resilience I hadn't yet learned to name.

For Your Reflection

1. Think of someone who taught you life lessons in an unconventional way. What did they teach you that still guides you now?

_____

_____

_____

2. When in your life did you feel "poor" on paper but rich in love, wisdom, or experience?

_____

_____

_____

3. What "armor" did your caregivers or elders give you? Skills, sayings, habits, or beliefs that still protect you?

_____

_____

_____

Affirmations to Hold Onto

- I carry the wisdom of those who came before me, even if they didn't have perfect words or perfect lives.

- I am capable, resourceful, and guided by lessons that live in my bones.

**Even Broken Love Leave Lessons
That Help Us Grow into Ourselves.**

Chapter 3
THE RETURN I NEVER WANTED

When my mother came back for me, it felt like my whole world was ending. I loved living with Grandpa. I was accustomed to our slow, familiar routines. Accompanying him to doctor appointments, taking long walks to the grocery store, and stopping on the way back so he could visit his late wife's grave and tell me stories about life, love, and everything in between. With him, life made sense.

I knew my mother, but not with the kind of memories a child treasures. Her addiction and criminal history were the shadows that followed her. When she asked if I wanted to come live with her, I told her no and said I wanted to stay with Grandpa. She got upset and told me I had to go, anyway. I suppose it was court-approved; Grandpa was getting older, and she had already regained custody of my sister, who was just a few years older than me.

Leaving Grandpa's one-bedroom housing project apartment, the only stability I knew, and moving into a brownstone downtown with my mother and her Irish/Italian boyfriend was jarring. It was an upgrade in appearance, but emotionally, it felt like I was stepping into another world. One I didn't trust. One I didn't understand. One I wasn't sure had room for me.

Everything felt strange at first: new house, new rules, new energies I didn't quite trust. My mom had a laugh that could fill a whole room, and when she was good, she was magic. She could light up a space with one smile. But when the darkness came, when the cravings hit or the sadness weighed her down, it was like watching a light flicker until it wasn't sure it wanted to shine at all.

There were nights she disappeared for hours, sometimes days. I'd find my older sister waiting by the window, watching for our mother to come home. I'd tell her to go to bed, trying to reassure her and myself that everything would be okay. That she was okay. That she loved us. And she loved me. Just not always in the ways I needed. Addiction doesn't leave much room for consistency; it steals the best parts of people and makes you question whether love is enough to hold onto.

Still, I saw beautiful parts of her. Her humor. Her strength. The way she could make anyone laugh. The way she fought silently, even when she didn't win. There was always a part of me that believed she was trying, fighting to be the mother she wanted to be. And when she called me her miracle baby, I felt it. Deep.

Sometimes she'd talk about the baby she lost, my twin, and a distant look would wash over her face. "You were the one who made it," she'd say softly, brushing my hair back. "God kept you here for a reason." I used to nod like I understood, but now I think she saw a strength in me long before I ever recognized it in myself.

Life with my mom wasn't easy, but it shaped me. I learned to read moods before I learned to read books. I learned how to take care of myself, and sometimes how to take care of her too. I learned that love could be broken and still be real.

Even in the chaos, she was teaching me something: how to survive, how to adapt, how to find beauty in the middle of the storm.

That's why I can't tell my story without telling hers. Because even in her struggle, my mother gave me something priceless: the will to keep going, the tenderness to love deeply, and the belief that miracles

15

don't always happen before you begin the fight. Sometimes the miracle is that you survived long enough to create one of your own.

For Your Reflection

1. How has addiction, mental health, or instability shown up in your family story, and how did it shape your view of love?

_____

_____

_____

2. What conflicting truths did you hold about your mother, father, or caregivers at the same time (loving them and being hurt by them)?

_____

_____

_____

3. If you could tell your younger self one thing about your mother or caregiver, what would it be?

_____

_____

_____

Affirmations to Hold Onto

- I am allowed to hold both love and pain when I think about my family.

- Their struggles are part of my story, but they are not my destiny.

Sometimes The Truth Arrives Late, But Right on Time for Your Healing.

Chapter 4
THE TRUTH ABOUT MY FATHER

I always knew my father. He wasn't some mystery figure who showed up out of nowhere one day. His name lived in whispers and half-finished conversations. But what I didn't know, what no one ever told me, was the truth.

My father was also my oldest sister's father. My mother met him when she was eighteen and he was twenty-five, a married musician she met at a bar. What was meant to be a one-night encounter became my sister. And somehow, that connection kept pulling them back to each other. I think once my mother found out she was pregnant, what started as a mistake turned into something that felt like fate... or maybe unfinished business.

Their relationship continued for years, complicated and secret. Eventually, she grew tired of being a mistress. She married someone new, started a family, had my two middle siblings, and then me, the last of her four children.

For as long as I could remember, I had been told that a different man was my father. I believed it because children believe what they are told. Why wouldn't I?

But life has a way of revealing truth on its own timeline.

After moving back in with my mother, I had an encounter with my sister's father, the man I'd always known as *her* dad. He looked at me and asked, "Did your mother ever tell you that I'm your father?"

I stared at him, confused, and said, "No."

When I got home, I told my mother what he had said, expecting her to laugh or explain. Instead, her face hardened.

"He's lying," she snapped. "Don't believe him."

I didn't ask again. But something about the moment stayed with me. Her tone, the way she looked away, the heaviness in the silence.

Months later, I needed money for school. I told her I didn't have what I needed. She sighed, scribbled a number on a scrap of paper, and handed it to me.

"Call your father," she said. "Tell him he needs to help you."

I froze. Call my father?

She didn't explain. Just waved me off.

So, there I was, standing at the pay phone downstairs, holding that small piece of paper like a question I wasn't ready to ask. When the voice on the other end said, "Hello," I recognized it immediately.

It was him.

"My mother said you're my father," I blurted out. "And you need to pay for my school stuff."

There was a long pause. Then he said gently, "I'll be by tomorrow."

And he was.

He showed up the next day, handed me the money, and said he wanted to start picking me up on Fridays after school. True to his word, he came every Friday and brought me back home on Sundays after church.

Did I mention my father was a pastor?

Yes, the same man who once lived deep in addiction found his way back to God, got clean, and became a pastor. Life has a strange way of writing stories none of us could make up.

At first, I was scared of him. He was a stranger, and I didn't know how to trust, this truth that had been kept from me for so long. But those weekends slowly became sacred. Sometimes we rode in silence, the hum of the car filling in the spaces between us. Other times, we'd sit for hours after church, sharing stories, laughing, and rebuilding years that secrecy had stolen.

Eventually, my family moved next door to him, and our relationship deepened. He remained consistent, showing up, calling, and checking on me. After my mother passed, our bond grew even stronger. I needed him in a way I hadn't allowed myself before.

I started planning our daddy–daughter dates. I asked him about everything: his childhood, his dreams, his regrets, his faith. I didn't just want to know who my father was. I wanted to know the man he had become.

Even after I moved to Georgia, if he called asking to see me, I'd fly or drive back home.

"Baby," he'd say, "let's have one of our dates."

And I'd be there. Every single time.

His presence became my healing. My closure. My peace.

Losing him hurt in a way different from losing my mother. Both losses broke me, but his felt softer. Maybe because this time, I wasn't left with unanswered questions. I got to tell him I loved him. I forgave him. I thanked him for showing up, finally, fully, in the way only he could.

When my mother died, I drowned myself in alcohol, crying myself to sleep for months. But by the time I lost my father, I had learned better ways to grieve. Therapy taught me that healing doesn't mean forgetting; it means letting yourself feel the loss without letting it destroy you.

My father's death hurt deeply, but it didn't undo me. Because by then, I understood something only lived experience can teach:

Sometimes, the people who break you early are the same ones who help put you back together in the end.

For Your Reflection

1. What "family secrets" or unspoken truths have impacted how you see yourself?

2. Have you ever had to rebuild a relationship from the ground up? What did that healing look like?

3. When you think of your parents or guardians now, what do you most want to remember—and what do you choose to release?

Affirmations to Hold Onto

- I am worthy of truth, even if it arrives late.

- I am allowed to grieve what I didn't receive and still embrace the love that eventually showed up.

PART II

INTRODUCTION: LOSS, BECOMING & BREAKING CYCLES

This section is about transition. The seasons in life when everything you thought was permanent falls apart, and you're left standing in the middle of the pieces, trying to decide what can still be saved.Here is where I learned the languages of grief, endurance, and reinvention.

Where I discovered that becoming stronger doesn't mean hardening, it means softening enough to grow. Part II holds the chapters where I stopped inheriting patterns and started rewriting them.

Grief Breaks You Open, But It Also Reveals Who You Are Becoming.

Chapter 5
LOSING MOM AND DAD TOO SOON

I thought I knew what loss was until I lost my parents.

When my mother passed away, it felt like the ground beneath me split open. She wasn't just my mom. She was my son's best friend, my daily phone call, the person I reached for without thinking. And even though our relationship carried its own scars, she understood me in a way no one else ever could.

She was only in her fifties.

I was thirty-one. My son was five.

Watching him struggle to understand where his nanna went was almost as painful as facing the loss myself. I had to be strong for him when all I wanted to do was fall apart.

After she died, I no longer recognized myself. Nights were the hardest. The quiet made everything louder. I'd pour a drink to silence the ache, then another to silence the memory of the first. I told myself it was coping, but it was really drowning. I was trying to numb a pain that felt too big to carry.

And in that fog, I lost my faith.

I remember sitting in church one Sunday and feeling absolutely nothing. The hymns that once comforted me were suddenly hollow.

The prayers felt unanswered. I kept asking,

How can there be a God?

What did I do to deserve so much hurt?

I had already survived childhood trauma, heartbreak, single motherhood, and loss. But losing my mother broke something sacred in me. It wasn't just grief. It felt like a betrayal. I trusted that faith would protect me from pain, and when it didn't, I didn't know where to put the anger.

And then, just as I began to find my footing again, life struck a second time.

I lost my father when I was thirty-six.

Losing him was different. We had rebuilt a relationship that had been denied to us for so many years. We talked often, laughed, went on our daddy–daughter dates, and made up for lost time. When he died, it hurt deeply, but it was a gentler pain, because this time, I wasn't left with regrets. I told him everything I needed to say. I loved him fully, and he loved me back.

But even with that peace, the ache remained.

It wasn't just losing two parents.

It was losing the people who shaped the beginning of my story.

For a long time, I carried anger not only toward God, but toward life itself. Every prayer I tried to say came out as a question:

Why me? Why so much? Why now?

But grief has a way of becoming a teacher. Over time, it softened me again. Therapy helped. Writing helped. Talking about them helped. Slowly, I learned that faith isn't about never questioning, it's about still reaching for hope even when the answers don't come.

I still miss them every day. I still reach for the phone out of habit. I still hear my father's laugh in moments that catch me off guard. But I've learned something sacred:

Their love didn't leave with them. It lives through me, and through my son.

Losing both of my parents broke my heart, but it also revealed my purpose. Because even in the middle of all that loss, something inside me whispered:

You're still here. Keep going.

And somehow, I did.

For Your Reflection

1. How has grief shown up in your body, routines, or beliefs?

   _____

   _____

   _____

2. What did you lose when your loved one died, and what did you gain in wisdom, perspective, or purpose?

   _____

   _____

   _____

3. Has grief ever shifted or challenged your faith or spirituality? Where are you with that now?

_____

_____

_____

Affirmations to Hold Onto

- My grief is a reflection of my love, and both are valid.

- I can question, wrestle, and still find my way back to hope.

You Are Allowed to Rewrite the Story Your Family Handed You.

Chapter 6
BREAKING CYCLES, BUILDING DREAMS

Track and field saved my life.

I didn't walk onto that track chasing trophies or titles; I just wanted to know what it felt like to run toward something instead of away from it. When I entered high school, one of my childhood friends told me she was joining her school's track team to earn a college scholarship. I hadn't thought that far ahead; college felt like something that happened to other people. But I figured, *why not?* So, I signed up too.

It turned out I was actually pretty good. Running came naturally. The rhythm of my breath, the pound of my feet against the track; it felt like freedom. Every lap was a release. All the noise, the chaos, the pain I didn't know how to process, it all fell away when I ran.

And then came Ms. Kennedy, my high school coach. I called her Sista, because that's what she felt like to me, family. She didn't just coach me; she *saw* me. She saw the tired eyes behind the smile, the kid carrying too much too soon. Sista poured into me like her belief alone could fill every gap life had carved into me.

She pushed me harder than anyone ever had, but she also cared in a way I wasn't used to. She signed me up for SAT prep classes when no one else was thinking about college for me. She made sure I had running shoes that actually fit, snacks for track meets, and pep talks for the days I doubted myself.

"You can get out, Angela," she used to say. "You can go somewhere."

And I did.

When Sista retired, her husband stepped in as coach, and somehow the care continued. They came to see me off when I accepted an out-of-state scholarship, hugging me like proud parents. Later, they even visited me at college, cheering me on from the stands like I was their own.

Track gave me hope. It showed me that life existed beyond Jersey City, NJ, beyond everything I thought I was destined to be. It taught me that I could build something new for myself. That I could run toward a future instead of running from my past.

After graduating with my bachelor's degree, I realized I had broken a cycle that had lived in my family for generations. I was the first to graduate from college. The one who took all those painful beginnings and turned them into a different kind of story. It wasn't easy, but every practice, every early-morning meet, every word of encouragement from Sista reminded me that struggle didn't have to define me; it could refine me.

Track taught me endurance. And life would test that lesson again and again. But it also taught me something even deeper:

You don't have to be the fastest to win. Sometimes, you just have to keep showing up at the starting line.

For Your Reflection

1. What cycles or patterns in your family did you decide (or are deciding now) to break?

   _____

   _____

   _____

2. Who believed in your potential before you fully saw it in yourself? How did their belief change you?

   _____

   _____

   _____

3. When have you felt most free? Physically, emotionally, or spiritually? What contributed to that feeling?

   _____

   _____

   _____

Affirmations to Hold Onto

- I am a cycle breaker and dream builder.

- I deserve opportunities, open doors, and spaces where I can thrive.

Becoming Your Own Safe Place Is One of the Greatest Love Stories of All.

Chapter 7
LOVE, DIVORCE, AND LEARNING MYSELF AGAIN

I met my son's father during my first year of grad school. Things moved fast, too fast. Within a few months, we were pregnant and talking about marriage. Looking back, I know I was chasing stability, chasing the family I always longed for. But that chapter ended almost as quickly as it began.

When my son was born, everything shifted. Love stopped being about romance and became about responsibility, protection, and purpose. He became my entire world, the reason I worked harder, the reason I kept going even when I was exhausted. But motherhood also made me cautious. I wasn't sure I'd ever open my heart again. Love felt risky. I had built walls so high that even I couldn't see over them sometimes.

Still, I tried.

I dated again, slowly. Some connections ended because I was too guarded. Others ended because I knew they weren't aligned with who I was becoming. I confused companionship with connection more than once. Each time I walked away, I did so with a little more clarity. Being alone didn't mean I was unloved. It meant I was learning not to settle for less than I deserved.

Then came my ex-husband. What began with promise and steadiness eventually unraveled. There were many reasons, but they're not what defines that season for me. What matters is what I learned: every relationship taught me something about myself, my boundaries, and the kind of love I truly need. For that, I am grateful.

Motherhood has never been easy, but it has been my greatest teacher. My son has seen more than most children his age. He was five when my mother, his nanna and best friend, passed away. Eleven when my marriage ended. Twelve when my father died. And then, as if life had not tested him enough, he had to watch me battle breast cancer, trying to stay strong for him even when fear was swallowing me whole.

There were nights I would peek into his room, watching him sleep, and whisper silent prayers that one day he would understand and see his mother not as someone who had it all together, but as someone who kept trying. For him. For herself. For the life we both deserved.

I think he understands now. We talk more. We laugh more. We dream out loud about the future. And every time I see his smile, I'm reminded that love didn't fail me. It simply took on a new shape. It became the quiet strength that lives inside both of us.

Because love isn't just about who stays. It's about what remains.

For Your Reflection

1. When you look back at your relationships, what were you seeking? Safety, validation, companionship, healing, or something else?

_____

_____

_____

2. In what ways have you settled for less than you deserved? What are your non-negotiables now?

_____

_____

_____

3. How has motherhood, caregiving, or loving someone deeply reshaped your definition of love?

_____

_____

_____

Affirmations to Hold Onto

- I am allowed to start over in love, including the way I love myself.

- Being alone does not mean I am unlovable; it means I am choosing alignment over settling.

Some Hearts Are Called to Hold Others, Even While Mending Themselves.

Chapter 8
HOLDING SPACE FOR OTHERS

I became a crisis responder nine years ago, and I can honestly say it changed me. It's one thing to survive your own storms, but it's another to sit in the middle of someone else's and help them find their way out.

But my path into this work didn't start with crisis lines. I've been in the helping profession since 2002, long before I ever picked up a headset.

I earned my MSW and built a career serving people in every corner of the community.

As a community consultant, a social worker, an assessment counselor, a community care therapist, and a substance abuse counselor. Every role taught me something different about humanity. Every person I worked with shaped the way I see the world.

But crisis work… that was different.

When I first started, I thought it would be another chapter in my career. Another way to help people. Another extension of purpose. But I learned quickly that crisis work isn't just a job; it's a calling. Every call is different. Every voice carries a story. And every silence is a scream that only someone who's lived through pain can truly understand.

I've spoken with veterans, mothers, teenagers, elders, and people standing right at the edge of giving up. I've stayed on the line for hours with strangers, reminding them there is still life left to live, even when it doesn't feel like it. Some nights, after I hang up, I sit in the quiet and pray for the voices I'll never hear again.

Crisis work has shown me the best and worst of humanity. It's taught me more about compassion than any classroom ever could. I've learned that sometimes the most powerful thing you can do for someone is listen. Not a fix. Not lecture. Not rescue. Just listen.

Being a crisis responder forced me to reflect on my own story, too. There are moments when a caller's grief or fear echoes my own past: loss, survival, loneliness, the weight of being strong for everyone around you. It's humbling. It's healing. It's hard.

After my breast cancer diagnosis, there were nights I wondered how I could keep holding space for others while trying not to fall apart myself. But strangely, the calls kept me steady. They reminded me that survival is universal; that we are all trying to make it to the next sunrise, one breath at a time.

The empathy that once felt heavy eventually became what strengthened me. It's what connects me to people, in crisis, in community, in life. Through every voice I've sat with, I've learned that pain doesn't discriminate. But neither does hope.

Looking back, I realized crisis work wasn't something I stumbled into; it was something my life prepared me for. Every role, every lesson, every heartache, every healing moment, my entire journey shaped me into the woman who could sit with someone else's darkness without being swallowed by it.

Nine years later, I'm still here.

Still answering the phone.

Still believing in people.

Still holding space.

And maybe that's the greatest gift this work has given me: the reminder that healing isn't a destination. It's a daily practice, one conversation, one connection, one act of grace at a time.

For Your Reflection

1. In what ways do you hold space for others? In your work, family, friendships, or community?

_____

_____

_____

2. Where do you feel most drained, and where do you feel most fulfilled when supporting others?

_____

_____

_____

3. How can you offer yourself the same compassion and patience you give to everyone else?

_____

_____

_____

Affirmations to Hold Onto

- I am a safe place for others, and I am learning to be a safe place for myself.

- I can care deeply for others without abandoning my own needs.

PART III

INTRODUCTION: SURVIVING THE FIGHT

This is the season where life demanded everything of me, mind, body, and spirit.

Part III is where breast cancer entered my story, not as a villain, but as a catalyst. A force that stripped away what I thought defined me and revealed who I truly was beneath it all.

These chapters chronicle the fight for my body, the rediscovery of my beauty, and the rebirth of my purpose.

This part is survival but more than that, it's awakening.

Your Spirit Can Rise Even When Your Body Is Weary.

Chapter 9
WHEN THE BODY BETRAYS YOU

I thought I had known fear before, but nothing prepares you for the moment someone looks you in the eyes and says, "You have breast cancer and it's covering 80% of your breast."

After my breast specialist confirmed what the lab tech had told me over the phone, I remember sitting in the room in complete shock. Everything blurred. The walls, the doctor's words, the world I thought I knew; all of it dissolved into a thick, unbreathable silence. I tried to hold it together, but the tears came before I could stop them. I didn't know what to think, what to say, or even how to breathe.

The first person I called was my son's father. I could barely get the words out.

"They said it's breast cancer," I whispered through tears.

There was a pause, one that felt like the whole world had stopped. Then his voice came through, firm and steady, the kind of voice you lean into when you're falling apart.

"Cut out all that crying," he said gently but firmly. "You're going to beat this. You're going to be okay. David still needs you, and I do too."

Something in me steadied when he said that. I didn't fully believe it yet, but I wanted to for my son. For the life I still had to live.

After I hung up, I called my cousin. We didn't talk; we just cried together, sharing the kind of silence that only people who love you deeply can hold. Sometimes there are no right words, only presence.

That night, I lay in bed thinking about everything, my son, my parents, my past, my future.

For a moment, it felt like life had betrayed me. After everything I had already survived, how could this be happening? I kept thinking, *Haven't I fought enough battles already?*

But even in that darkness, light began to show up, in the form of my village.

My sisters and friends stepped in like an army of love. They researched treatments, showed up at appointments, cooked meals, cleaned my home, and made sure I never fought alone. They bought me comfort gifts: soft blankets, inspirational books, herbal teas, candles, anything they thought might bring warmth into the coldest season of my life.

My son's father and his family also took care of me. They stepped in to make sure David was okay when I couldn't be. Their quiet, dependable support reminded me that healing never happens alone. It happens in the community.

Breast cancer humbled me. It stripped away every illusion of control and revealed what truly mattered: faith, family, and the people who show up when you have nothing left to give.

There were nights when I'd look in the mirror: bald head, tired eyes, scars mapping a story I never asked to write and whisper to myself:
You're still here. You're still fighting.

And I did fight.

For myself.

For David.

For my parents' legacy.

For every woman who has ever had to rebuild herself piece by piece.

Breast Cancer may have changed my body, but it uncovered my spirit. It showed me that even when the body betrays you, the soul can rise fiercely, beautifully, and full of hope.

For Your Reflection

1. When have you felt disconnected from your body? Through illness, trauma, shame, or exhaustion?

   _____

   _____

   _____

2. How did you respond when your body changed in ways you didn't choose?

   _____

   _____

   _____

3. What would it look like to treat your body as a partner instead of an enemy?

   _____

   _____

   _____

Affirmations to Hold Onto

- My body's scars and changes are evidence of battles that I survived, not beauty lost.

- Even when my body feels fragile, my spirit is allowed to be fierce.

I Survived the Storm, But I Carry the Names of the Ones Who Didn't.

Chapter 10
SURVIVORS' REMORSE

I didn't know survivor's remorse was a real thing until I felt it in my bones.

People think surviving breast cancer is the end of the pain, the final victory lap after months of fighting, bleeding, breaking, healing, and praying. They imagine that when the doctor finally says, "no evidence of disease," the world becomes soft again. They think the story ends with relief, celebration, and second chances.

But survival comes with questions.

With ghosts. With losses that sit beside you even while you're still breathing.

And no one prepared me for the guilt of living.

There were days in treatment when I could barely stand, when I felt my body changing in ways I never wanted to imagine. But even in that pain, I knew I wasn't alone. One of my closest cousins, Marjorie, wasn't just family; we were thick as thieves from childhood, way into adulthood. We shared secrets, laughs, memories, and a kind of closeness that didn't require explanation.

When Marjorie passed away right after my first round of chemo, my heart cracked in a place I didn't know existed. My best friend and my sister received the news before I did. They stood in my room and looked at me, weak, fighting nausea, pain, and fear, and they didn't know how to tell me.

They whispered to each other. They avoided my eyes. They carried the weight of that truth as if it was going to shatter me.

And when they finally spoke the words, something inside me broke. Not physically, this pain had nothing to do with breast cancer. It was the kind of grief that steals your breath.

I was fighting for my life while losing someone whose life meant everything to me.

That was the first time I wondered: Why am I still here? Why her and not me?

But it wasn't the last time I asked that question.

During my journey, I lost Mrs. Victoria, the woman whose strength shaped Pink Hope's heartbeat. She lived with a kind of grace that didn't need an audience. Losing her felt like losing one of the pillars holding me up. We shared dreams of life after cancer, joy, and purpose, and cancer stole that from her.

Then there was Fajr, the little warrior I never met in person, but immediately felt connected to. I watched her grow up through social media. Every year, I'd look forward to seeing what her birthday theme would be, even though her mom always claimed she wasn't having a party. And every year, without fail, the party came, bigger, brighter, and more magical than the last.

Fajr, diagnosed with Osteosarcoma, went into the treatment rooms with a smile that didn't belong to someone fighting for her life. Her innocence and joy humbled me. If she could smile, how could I complain? Watching her courage made me push through my own pain, even on the days I wanted to give up.

And still… she didn't survive.

Her mother lost her only daughter. And I kept asking myself: Why me? Why did my body respond when hers didn't?

Then I lost Uncle Chuck, a man who constantly asked me how I did it, how I made it through the pain, how I kept going when everything in my body was changing. He'd look at me like I was stronger than I felt, like I had some secret formula for surviving.

His passing hit me in a quiet, aching way. The kind that sits in the back of your throat. The kind that doesn't soften with time.

And then… my beloved Mrs. Kennedy.

A woman who had already beaten cancer once, only to have it return years later. She fought with a faith that felt unshakeable. She believed. She hoped. She prayed.

And still… cancer took her.

By the time she passed, I felt surrounded by loss. It felt like every time I stood up, life handed me another reason to kneel.

And I kept thinking: Why am I here? What made me different? What made me the one who survived when the people I loved didn't?

Survivor's remorse is not just sadness.

It is guilt.

It is confusion.

It is waking up grateful and grieving at the same time.

It is smiling for your second chance while crying for the people who never got theirs.

It is realizing that survival is a blessing, but it is also a burden.

For a long time, I struggled to celebrate my milestones. I felt that honoring my life meant dishonoring theirs. But slowly, painfully, I learned something:

Survival isn't a comparison. It's a calling.

I didn't survive instead of them.

I survived because there is still work for me to do.

Still people for me to help.

Still hope for me to give.

Still lives for me to touch.

They are the reason.

They are the fire behind my purpose.

They are woven into Pink Hope's mission.

They are the voices in my heart whispering, "Keep going."

Survivor's remorse didn't disappear, but it transformed.

It became honor.

It became intention.

It became legacy.

It became my why.

I carry them with me every day, every milestone, every step.

My survival is meaningful because it includes their memory.

And as long as I am living… so are they.

For Your Reflection

1. What emotions arise when you think about surviving an experience that others did not?

_____

_____

_____

2. What does survivor's remorse look or feel like in your life?

_____

_____

_____

3. How can you honor the people you've lost through the way you live, give, and heal?

_____

_____

_____

Affirmations to Hold Onto

- I honor the ones I've lost by choosing to live fully and intentionally.

- My survival is not an accident; it is purpose.

- I am allowed to feel joy and grief at the same time. Both are holy.

Pretty Isn't Something You Wear It's Something You Remember.

Chapter 11
PRESERVING MY PRETTY

For a long time after treatment, I struggled to recognize the woman staring back at me in the mirror. The hair that once framed my face was gone. My skin carried reminders of chemo and radiation. My scars told stories I never asked to live through. I'd tilt my head and wonder, *Who is she now?*

I used to think "pretty" was about how I looked. My hair laid, nails polished, lip gloss perfect. But breast cancer changed that. It forced me to look for beauty in places I never thought to check: in survival, in resilience, in the quiet moments when I showed up for myself even when I didn't feel like it.

One morning, after another restless night, I caught my reflection and, for the first time, I didn't zero in on what I'd lost. I saw something new: light. Not the old kind but the kind that comes after you've walked through darkness. The kind that whispers, *You're still here.*

In that moment, I realized that preserving my pretty wasn't about holding on to who I was before breast cancer. It was about honoring the woman I had become because of it.

Pink Hope Boutique and the Pink Hope Foundation grew from that revelation. They aren't just businesses; they're reflections of my healing. Every garment, every head wrap, every detail is intentional. They are love letters to every woman trying to rediscover her confidence, reminding us all that beauty never truly disappears and sometimes it just waits beneath the pain for us to uncover it again.

I started redefining "pretty" for myself. Pretty became:

- Showing up to treatment with a bold scarf and a brave heart.

- Smiling through the fear because joy was worth fighting for.

- Loving the body that fought to keep me alive.

- Choosing peace over perfection.

I learned that preserving your pretty means preserving your **power**. It means choosing to love yourself through every version of who you are: the broken, the healing, and the blooming.

As I began sharing this message through Pink Hope, something beautiful happened: women started sharing their stories back with me. Survivors. Thrivers. Caretakers. Daughters. Mothers. Each one reclaiming beauty in new ways. Because healing is never just about one person: it's a ripple effect.

Some days, I still have to remind myself that "pretty" isn't always polished. Sometimes it's puffy eyes from crying but still getting out of bed. Sometimes it's laughter breaking through the pain. Sometimes it's simply surviving today.

But I'm learning that preserving your pretty isn't about staying the same.
It's about staying true

Because beauty fades, hair falls out, and bodies change, but grace, resilience, and faith? Those are timeless.

And I carry those now as my truest form of pretty.

For Your Reflection

1. What did "pretty" or "attractive" mean to you growing up, and how has that meaning evolved?

   _____

   _____

   _____

2. How has illness, trauma, or change attempted to redefine your beauty — and how are you reclaiming it now?

   _____

   _____

   _____

3. What small practices, rituals, or acts help you feel most like yourself?

   _____

   _____

   _____

Affirmations to Hold Onto

- My pretty is my power, and it lives in my spirit, not my reflection.

- I honor every version of myself: the broken, the healing, and the blooming.

PART IV

INTRODUCTION: PURPOSE, LEGACY & BECOMING

The final part of this memoir is where the pieces come together, where pain transforms into purpose, where resilience becomes legacy, and where becoming is no longer a struggle but a calling.

These chapters celebrate the woman I am now and the mission that grew from my scars.

Part IV honors the truth that healing is not a destination; it is a lifelong unfolding.

This is where hope blossoms into something bigger than me, something rooted in love, service and faith.

Purpose Often Blooms from the Places That Once Hurt the Most.

Chapter 12
THE BIRTH OF PINK HOPE

Breast cancer didn't just change my health; it changed my reflection.

I still remember sitting with my nurse as she went over the long list of side effects from my chemo medications: hair loss, fatigue, skin changes, weight gain, nail discoloration, and more. I listened quietly, nodding at each one, until finally I blurted out:

"Oh, so I'm going to be ugly?"

For a split second, she looked startled. Then we both burst into laughter. The kind that comes from fear, disbelief, and the desperate need to lighten something too heavy to hold.

But when the laughter faded, and I was alone later, I remember thinking,
What if that's true? What if I don't recognize myself anymore?

And truthfully, I didn't.

Not for a long time.

Chemo changed everything.

The rash.

The weight gain.

The "chemo teeth."

The scars.

The swelling.

The fatigue.

All of it chipped away at how I saw myself. I'd look in the mirror and feel like a stranger was staring back at me. I didn't feel pretty anymore. I didn't feel powerful. I didn't feel like me.

Some days, I avoided my reflection altogether.Other days, I'd stand there and quietly grieve the woman I used to be.

And then I'd wonder about the other women in the chemo chairs beside me.

Were they mourning their reflection too?

Were they missing the version of themselves they thought they'd never see again?

That's when the seed for Pink Hope Boutique was planted.

I've always believed that when you look good, you feel good. But during treatment, that belief became a matter of survival. I started noticing how limited recovery clothing options were. Everything looked so sterile, so clinical, so unlike *us*. We were women still living, still fighting, still showing up in bodies we barely recognized: yet everything designed for us seemed to forget that.

Why did healing have to look and feel so stripped down? Why should we have to choose between comfort and confidence?

I thought, why should healing mean giving up our style?

So, I decided I wanted to create something different. Something soft but stylish, functional yet fashionable. I wanted to design pieces that honored both comfort and confidence, garments that helped women preserve their dignity through the hardest chapter of their lives. Because beauty doesn't end with diagnosis; it simply changes shape.

That's how Pink Hope Boutique was born.

It started as an idea in the middle of my healing, part therapy, part rebellion. Every design of head wraps, every cozy garment, every thoughtful accessory became a reminder that we deserve to feel beautiful, even in the fight. That we deserve to look in the mirror and still see someone worth celebrating.

And as the boutique grew in my heart, something bigger began to take shape too, The Pink Hope Foundation.

Where the boutique would help women reclaim their *outer beauty*, the foundation would help them heal from the *inside out*.

The foundation would focus on emotional support, mental wellness, community connections, and the kind of care you can't always see but always feel. It's hope with purpose. A space for women to be seen, supported, and celebrated in every stage of recovery.

Pink Hope isn't just a brand.

It's a movement.

A love letter to every woman rebuilding herself.

Born from laughter in a hospital room, and from the courage to find "pretty" in the middle of pain.

Because even when my body felt weak, my spirit didn't. And when I realized that I knew exactly what my purpose was:

To help other women, see that they are still beautiful, still strong, and still worthy, scars and all.

For Your Reflection

1. How has your reflection, physical or emotional, changed during your hardest seasons? What did those changes reveal about who you truly are?

_____

_____

_____

2. What moment in your life made you question your beauty, confidence, or identity? How did you rebuild from that place?

_____

_____

_____

3. Where do you see gaps in care, comfort, dignity, or support for women (or people) experiencing hardship? What part of you feel called to fill those spaces?

_____

_____

_____

4. What would it look like to create something that helps others feel seen, valued, or beautiful, even when life has changed their bodies or their circumstances?

_____

_____

_____

Affirmations to Hold Onto

- I am worthy of beauty, confidence, and comfort at every stage of my journey.

- My pain has a purpose, and I can transform it into something healing and powerful.

- I honor the parts of me that changed and the strength that rose in their place.

- Even when my reflection shifts, my worth remains unshakable.

A Legacy Isn't Built in What You Keep, But in What You Grow Through.

Chapter 13
LEGACY IN BLOOM

When I look back on my life, every twist, every heartbreak, every miracle, I see a garden that grew out of storms. For years, I thought the pain was punishment. Now, I know it was preparation.

Legacy isn't built in the easy seasons.

It's shaped in the moments when life forces you to start over and you choose to keep going, anyway.

My greatest legacy will always be my son. From the moment I heard his first cry, he became my reason to rise. He's watched me at my lowest and my strongest, through loss, heartbreak, rebuilding, and healing. Somehow, even when I struggled to believe in myself, he never stopped believing in me.

He's seen things no child should ever have to witness: his mother grieving, navigating divorce, fighting through chemo, radiation, surgery after surgery, and still showing up for life. For years, I worried about how that would shape him. But now I see what it created: a young man with a kind heart, a steady spirit, and a deep understanding of resilience.

I hope that when he looks back, he doesn't just see the pain, but he sees the perseverance. That he understands strength doesn't mean never breaking; it means finding the courage to rebuild.

My legacy also lives through **Pink Hope**.

Through every woman who walks into our space feeling broken and leaves standing taller.

Through every survivor who looks in the mirror and sees beauty again.

Through every family we touch, every story we honor, every life we remind that hope still lives here.

And, of course, my legacy lives through **Victoria**. The woman whose strength lit the first spark. The one who told me, "Start fighting now." Her spirit is woven into every part of Pink Hope.

The **Queen Victoria Grant** ensures her courage continues to shine, reminding others that love, when rooted in purpose, never dies. It multiplies.

There was a time I lost my faith. When grief felt heavier than belief and darkness felt louder than hope. But somewhere along this journey, I found it again. Not in pews or sermons, but in quiet gratitude... in laughter after tears... in the steady truth that love doesn't end.

My story isn't perfect. It's messy, painful, beautiful, and honest. But it's mine, and I'm proud of it.

Every scar tells a story.

Every tear watered something that eventually bloomed.

And every woman I meet reminds me why I'm still here: to keep planting hope, one heart at a time.

If I've learned anything, it's this:

Healing doesn't erase the past; it transforms it.

It turns wounds into wisdom and pain into purpose.

So, when I think about my legacy, it's not defined by what I've lost but by what I've built from it.

And as long as I'm here, I'll keep reminding others that no matter what life takes from you, you still have the power to preserve your pretty, fight for your joy, and bloom anyway.

Because hope, **Pink Hope**, always finds a way.

For Your Reflection

1. When people speak your name years from now, what do you want them to feel?

    _____

    _____

    _____

2. Who are the people, places, or communities that already carry pieces of your legacy?

    _____

    _____

    _____

3. If your younger self could see who you've become, what would she be most proud of?

    _____

    _____

    _____

Affirmations to Hold Onto

- My life is a garden, and even the storms have watered something beautiful.

- I am planting seeds of hope, healing, and faith that will outlive me.

Becoming Is the Quiet Miracle That Happens After Survival.

Chapter 14
THE POWER OF BECOMING

There was a time when I thought my story was only about survival, about making it through pain, heartbreak, loss, and illness. But now I see it was always about *becoming.*

Becoming stronger.

Becoming softer.

Becoming more grounded, more open, more whole.

Becoming the woman, I was always meant to be.

Every experience, from being born into chaos to standing in a hospital gown hearing the word breast cancer, was preparing me for this moment. For a life lived boldly. For a heart that loves deeply. For a purpose rooted in serving others who are still finding their way through the dark.

I used to think my scars were reminders of what I had lost. Now I understand they're evidence of what I survived, and what I gained: endurance, empathy, clarity, and purpose.

That's the heart of **Preserving My Pretty**. It's not just a story about breast cancer or grief or hardship. It's a story about rediscovering beauty in broken places and choosing, again and again, to show up for yourself, even when it hurts, even when you're tired, even when you're scared.

If my journey teaches you anything, I hope it's this:

You can be soft and still be strong. You can be scared and still be brave. You can lose everything and still create something beautiful from what remains.

Because healing isn't just what happens *to* you. It's what happens *through* you.

And my healing?

It bloomed into **Pink Hope**, a movement, a mission, a reminder that even after the hardest storms, beauty still grows.

I am still becoming. And so are you. And there is no timeline, no destination, only the promise that every day offers a new chance to rise, to choose yourself, and to uncover the parts of you that survived the fire.

Preserving my pretty didn't just save me.

It revealed me.

And I hope, in some gentle way, it helps reveal you to yourself too.

For Your Reflection

1. In what ways are *you* still becoming? Spiritually, emotionally, creatively, or professionally?

_____

_____

_____

2. What old versions of yourself are you ready to release with love and gratitude?

_____

_____

_____

3. If fear, guilt, or comparison couldn't speak, what would your next chapter look like?

_____

_____

_____

Affirmations to Hold Onto

- I am not finished; I am still becoming more of who I was created to be.

- Healing isn't behind me or ahead of me; it is unfolding within me right now.

Epilogue
AND STILL, I RISE

If you're holding this book in your hands, it means you've walked with me through the quiet places, the bruised places, the beautiful and broken places that shaped my life. And for that, I am grateful.

Writing this memoir was more than storytelling; it was a surrender. It was truth-telling. It was giving language to parts of my journey I once survived in silence. And somewhere between the first word and the last, I realized something important:

Healing doesn't end. It evolves.

There will always be new chapters, new lessons, new versions of ourselves waiting to emerge. Life will continue to surprise us with joy, challenge us with pain, and strengthen us with every step we take toward becoming.

If you are reading this because you've lived through your own storms. Loss, illness, heartbreak, trauma, identity shifts, please know this:

You are not alone. You are not broken. You are becoming.

And even when life feels unfamiliar, even when your reflection changes, even when you question everything you thought you knew... There is still something beautiful ahead, something blooming quietly beneath the surface, waiting for you to notice it.

Pink Hope is my offering to the world, a reminder that beauty doesn't end with struggle, and that purpose often grows where the heart has been cracked open.

So, wherever you are in your journey, healing, rebuilding, rediscovering yourself, I hope this story whispers gently to you:

Preserve your pretty.

Protect your peace.

Choose yourself.

And rise anyway.

My story continues. Yours does too.

And I pray that in some way, our paths leave each other holding more hope than we started with.

With love, faith, and gratitude, **Angela**

RESOURCES

Cancer Support Resources

American Cancer Society Information, transportation, lodging, and support groups. www.cancer.org

Susan G. Komen Foundation Education, community programs, and financial assistance. www.komen.org

Unite for HER Support services for women navigating breast cancer and wellness therapies (one of your real-life connections). www.uniteforher.org

Living Beyond Breast Cancer Support groups, conferences, and survivor education. www.lbbc.org

National Breast Cancer Foundation Patient navigation, early detection programs, online community. www.nationalbreastcancer.org

FajrStrOng, LLC Founded in memory of Fajr, this organization supports families affected by osteosarcoma through advocacy, awareness, and community resources.

MIB Agents (Make It Better) A national nonprofit dedicated to making it better for children and families impacted by osteosarcoma through research support, patient resources, education, and peer connections. https://mibagents.org

Prostate Cancer Foundation (PCF) Provides research funding, patient education, and early detection awareness for prostate cancer. https://www.pcf.org

No Stomach for Cancer A global organization focused on raising awareness, supporting research, and providing resources for individuals and families affected by stomach cancer. https://nostomachforcancer.org

Mental Health & Crisis Support

988 Suicide & Crisis Lifeline Immediate emotional support anytime. Call or text 988

Crisis Text Line Text HOME to 741741 for 24/7 support. www.crisistextline.org

Therapy for Black Girls Mental health directory and wellness resources. www.therapyforblackgirls.com

National Alliance on Mental Illness (NAMI) Education, peer groups, mental health advocacy. www.nami.org

Grief, Loss & Healing Support

GriefShare Local grief groups and support communities. www.griefshare.org

What's Your Grief Online articles, courses, and practical grief tools. www.whatsyourgrief.com

The Dougy Center Support for grieving children and teens. www.dougy.org

Women's Empowerment & Self-Worth Resources

The Body Positive Self-love, body acceptance, and confidence resources. www.thebodypositive.org

I AM Beautiful Foundation Community programs supporting women's empowerment. www.iambeautifulfoundation.org

Pink Hope Resources

Pink Hope Boutique @pink_hope_boutique Comfort, beauty, and confidence for women during recovery. (website "Coming 2026")

Pink Hope Foundation @pinkhopefoundation Emotional, spiritual, and community support for survivors, thrivers, and caretakers. (website "Launching Soon")

Queen Victoria Grant Honoring Victoria's legacy by supporting women rebuilding their lives with courage and grace. ("Coming 2026")

PROMPTS FOR SELF-DISCOVERY

1. Who are you today beyond your roles, responsibilities, and titles?

2. What moments in your life changed you the most for better or for growth?

3. In what areas of your life have you silenced your own needs?

4. What parts of your identity are you rediscovering or reclaiming?

5. What brings you joy that costs nothing?

6. What boundaries do you need to set to feel more whole?

7. When do you feel most like yourself?

8. What do you want to be remembered for?

9. What fears are you finally ready to release?

10. What is one truth about yourself you can no longer deny?

LETTERS TO YOUR YOUNGER SELF

To the Little Girl Who Survived More Than She Should Have

Prompts to guide your letter:

- What did she deserve to hear that no one said?
- What do you want her to know about the woman she becomes?
- What would you thank her for?
- What would you apologize to her for?

To the Teenager Who Didn't Know Her Power

Prompts:

- What insecurities was she carrying that were never hers to hold?
- What does she need to forgive herself for?
- What truth could have changed her entire world?

To the Woman You Were Before Life Broke You Open

Prompts:

- What do you wish she knew about love, worthiness, and resilience?
- What would you tell her about the storms she survived?
- How would you honor her strength?

Grief, Gratitude & Growth Pages

Prompts:

- What loss still lives quietly inside you?
- What emotions have you never given yourself permission to feel?
- Who or what do you need to release with love today?

Gratitude Pages

Prompts:

- List five small things that brought you peace this week.
- Who showed you kindness recently?
- What parts of yourself are you grateful for today?

Growth Pages

Prompts:

- What did life teach you this year?
- In what ways have you surprised yourself lately?
- What new strength have you discovered?

Vision Pages – "My Next Chapter"

If nothing was holding you back, what would your life look like one year from now?

What does healed, loved, whole YOU look like?

Prompts:

- What does she wear?

- How does she speak to herself?

- What does she no longer tolerate?

- What dreams does she finally allow herself to chase?

The Life You Are Becoming

Complete the statements:

- I am becoming a woman who…

  _____

- I am leaving behind…

  _____

- I am calling in…

  _____

- I am ready for…

  _____

The Hope List

A list for dreams, prayers, intentions, and quiet wishes you're calling into your life.

Prompts:

- What do you hope for your heart?

- What do you hope for your healing?

- What do you hope for your family?

- What do you hope for your purpose?

Your Hope List:

NOTES

(Full blank lined pages for journaling, ideas, and reflections.)

_____

_____

_____

_____

_____

_____

_____

_____

_____

_____

_____

_____

_____

_____

_____

_____

_____

_____

_____

_____

_____

_____

_____

_____